A WOODLAND MYSTERY™

The Buried Eye

A WOODLAND MYSTERY
By Irene Schultz

To doctors J. Alexander, R. Block, M. Canmann, S. Hamilton, R. Paul, and R. Sherman, who have added so much to my life

A Woodland Mystery

The Buried Eye
©1996 Story by Irene Schultz
Cover and cameo illustrations by Taylor Bruce
Interior illustrations by Merideth Yasui
Map illustration by Alicia Kramer
©1996 Wright Group Publishing, Inc.

Wright Group Development Team: Peter Beveridge, Marcie Bovetz, Katherine Campbell, Miriam Featherston, Karen Koll, Debra Lee, Karin Snelson, RV Stuckey, Rebel Williams

The Wright Group
19201 120th Avenue NE
Bothell, WA 98011

Printed in the United States of America

10 9 8 7 6 5 4 3 2 1

ISBN: 0-7802-7234-X

What family solves mysteries...has adventures all over the world...and loves oatmeal cookies?

It's the Woodlanders!

Sammy Westburg (10 years old)
His sister Kathy Westburg (13)
His brother Bill Westburg (14)
His best friend Dave Briggs (16)
His best grown-up friend Mrs. Tandy
And Mop, their little dog!

The children all lost their parents, but with Mrs. Tandy have made their own family.

Why are they called the Woodlanders? Because they live in a big house in the Bluff Lake woods. On Woodland Street!

Together they find fun, mystery, and adventure. What are they up to now?

Read on!

Meet the Woodlanders!

Sammy Westburg
Sammy is a ten-year-old wonder! He's big for his fifth-grade class, and big-mouthed, too. He has wild hair and makes awful spider faces. Even so, you can't help liking him.

Bill Westburg
Bill, fourteen, is friendly and strong, and only one inch taller than his brother Sammy. He loves Sammy, but pokes him to make him be quiet! He's in junior high.

Kathy Westburg
Kathy, thirteen, is small, shy, and smart. She wants to be a doctor someday! She loves to be with Dave, and her brothers kid her about it. She's in junior high, too.

Dave Briggs

Dave, sixteen, is tall and blond. He can't walk, so he uses a wheelchair and drives a special car. He likes coaching high-school sports, solving mysteries, and reading. And Kathy!

Mrs. Tandy

Sometimes the kids call her Mrs. T. She's Becky Tandy, their tall, thin, caring friend. She's always ready for a new adventure, and for making cookies!

Mop

Mop is the family's little tan dog. Sometimes they have to leave him behind with friends. But he'd much rather be running after Sammy.

Table of Contents

Chapter 1: Shining Eyes

Ten-year-old Sammy Westburg poked his older brother Bill on the arm.

He whispered, "When is the sun rise breakfast going to start? I'm starving.

And my legs are falling off!"

His whisper shot through the nearly dark museum. The crowd of people around him frowned.

Bill frowned at him, too.

So Sammy hit him. Then he ran behind a stone post.

The other three Woodlanders—Kathy, Dave Briggs, and Mrs. Tandy—were right next to the boys.

Mrs. Tandy looked at her watch and whispered softly, "We left Bluff Lake at four this morning. Now it's five thirty. No wonder Sammy's in a bad mood!"

Fourteen-year-old Bill whispered, "We all sort of are. And Sammy, king of pests, isn't helping any!"

They were all waiting for the museum's visitors from New Zealand to show up.

Suddenly they heard the sound of drums.

Sammy ran back over to Bill.

He said, "Somebody's coming out from behind the stuffed elephants! A Maori woman! From New Zealand!"

He said the word like this: MOW-er-ee, a little like FLOUR-ee. He had been practicing for a week.

Sixteen-year-old Dave said, "No, I bet she's an American Indian.

"I read that some of them would be meeting the Maoris here at the museum. Our first settlers, and New Zealand's first settlers. In the same room!"

The museum had invited its members ... along with American Indian and Maori guests ... for a special sunrise breakfast.

The museum wanted to thank the Maoris face-to-face for lending them some holy carvings.

The small American Indian woman walked out in front of the crowd. She was tapping on a little flat drum and singing.

Two other women followed her.

They wore deerskin dresses and bright robes of red, white, and black.

They were singing the same words over and over.

Sammy poked Bill AGAIN. He whispered, "Sounds like they're singing, 'HEY dee ... HEY dee ... HEY dee ... BLOSSom.'

"Is THIS what you guys woke me up at three in the morning to hear? HEY dee ... HEY dee ... HEY dee ... BLOSSom?

"Rotten rats! We haven't even seen one single Maori!

"I bet they never even got here from New Zealand. After all, it IS halfway around the world!"

Sammy's thirteen-year-old sister Kathy whispered, "It's OK, Sammy. They'll be here. And you're going to LOVE it!"

Then they heard another sound from behind the huge stuffed elephants.

Seven American Indian men danced out.

Sammy forgot to whisper. He said, "YIKES! What happened to THEM?"

They looked as tall as basketball players. And they all had animal heads.

Bill whispered, "They're wearing animal masks on top of their heads. Their own heads are inside the necks. That's why they look so tall."

5

Sammy said, "I knew that the whole time. I was asking to see if YOU knew."

Then, slowly, the big doors at the front of the main hall opened.

In a flash, twelve Maori men leaped through the doorway. Once inside, they never stopped moving. They danced from side to side, like wrestlers.

They even looked like wrestlers. They wore little bathing suits, with small black cloths hanging in the front and back.

They had carved stone shapes hanging from their necks.

They were barefoot.

Their muscles bulged out.

They were making awful faces, and their eyes bulged out.

They kept sticking their tongues straight out. Even their tongues bulged.

They waved long, heavy war clubs and grunted like bears.

They had knots of feathers in their hair and on their clubs.

They had black marks on their faces.

Sammy said, "Hey, why are they jumping like that ... with their legs apart ... and their knees bent out ... and their arms up?

"And why are they sticking their tongues in and out?   Like SNAKES!

"And listen to them grunt!

"What's happening?"

7

Dave said, "That's an old Maori way of scaring enemies. The American Indians are pretending to be their enemies."

Sammy said, "Look, the Maoris are puffing out their chests! They're dangerous!"

Bill said, "They're just faking it."

Sammy said, "Well, maybe it looks fake to YOU. But I wouldn't go NEAR one of those guys!"

The Maori war party pushed forward.

Then a dozen young Maori women walked into the museum. Their stiff grassy skirts made clicking noises.

Behind them came two hundred other Maoris ... dressed just like the museum crowd.

Mrs. Tandy whispered, "Those young women are beautiful! But the warriors! They don't seem to be pretending anymore. They seem ready to FIGHT!"

Sammy felt scared, and excited.

He started jumping up and down to the drum beat.

He started to sing, "HEY dee ... HEY dee ... HEY—"

Kathy whispered, "Better not do that, Sammy. They might think you're making fun of them."

Sammy said, "Boy, no one lets me do ANYTHING! I want to go home. And I'm not going with you guys on the trip to New Zealand next month, either."

Just then all the Maoris walked right past the American Indians and down the dark museum steps.

The whole museum crowd pushed forward after them. The Woodlanders were caught in the rush. They were pushed toward the stairs.

They had to keep going. They picked up Dave in his wheelchair and carried him down.

In the dimly lit basement, the Maoris stood facing a big wooden house.

Sammy took one look at it.

Then he grabbed hold of Bill's arm.

He held his breath.

His hair stood straight up.

HIS eyes bulged!

From the walls of the house, a hundred pairs of shining eyes were staring out at the crowd!

Chapter 2: Prisoner

The front of the house had wooden faces
carved all over it.

Every face had two huge, shining eyes.

Sammy held on to Bill's arm so hard

11

it hurt.

Bill said, "It's OK, Sammy. Those are just FAKE eyes. Carved out of sea shells. That's why they shine like that."

Some older Maori women walked up to the house. They patted it, as if it were a person. Then they started to cry.

Their hands began to shake, like leaves in the wind.

Sammy whispered, "What's wrong with them? Why are they doing that?"

Dave whispered, "The newspaper said that a hundred years ago, this house was sold by a money-hungry Maori from their tribe. A holy meeting house is never supposed to leave its tribe's land.

"Anyway, first it went to a museum in Europe. Then this museum bought it from that museum.

"After it was sold, the Maoris never saw it again ... until this moment."

Kathy said, "But why are they still so sad, now that they can see it?"

Dave said, "They're not. I think they're crying because they're happy. They believe the spirits of their dead ancestors live in those carvings. Now they can talk to those ancestors again."

Sammy said, "But why would they want to talk to their DEAD AUNT'S SISTERS? And why not their dead aunt's brothers?"

97-8539
1208539

Kathy laughed softly. "Not aunt's sisters, Sammy. AN-ces-tors. You know, great-grandparents, and great-great-grandparents who died a long time ago."

By now almost everybody was sitting down.

The older Maoris had chairs.

The younger ones sat on the floor.

The museum leaders had chairs.

But the Woodlanders and the rest of the museum crowd were left standing.

Sammy jabbed his elbow into Bill's ribs.

He whispered, "How come we have to stand up?"

Bill whispered, "I guess to show them respect ... to show we honor them and think they're important."

Sammy said, "Well, we've shown them enough respect. We've already respected them for an hour. Let's sneak out."

But by then the speech-making had begun. The Maori leaders spoke in the Maori language. They waved around heavy carved canes while they talked.

No one from the museum could understand what they were saying.

Sammy wiggled. He jiggled. He stood on one foot until it was tired. Then he tried the other foot.

Mrs. Tandy's shoes were too small. She whispered, "My feet are killing me!" She slipped out of her shoes and stood barefoot. She whispered, "I hope nobody notices!"

Bill whispered, "The Maori warriors would probably love it. They're barefoot, too!"

Then the museum leaders gave their speeches.

They said the people of the United States would always love the Maori house ... and would take care of it ... and would respect the Maoris' ancestors.

They announced that twenty American people were going to visit New Zealand ... to learn more about Maori people.

Sammy said, "Is THAT why we are going? I never knew that. Nobody ever tells me anything.

"I bet the Maoris HATE us. We are holding their ancestors prisoner in a stolen house in our museum basement!"

Dave laughed. He said, "Lucky thing this isn't a hundred years ago, and they DON'T hate us. They used to EAT people who were their enemies."

Sammy whispered, "You're kidding, Dave! You are, aren't you?"

Bill whispered, "Well, you can ask one of them at breakfast."

Sammy said, "Breakfast? You're going to have BREAKFAST with them? You must be crazy!"

By now the speeches were over.

The Maoris moved up the stairs.

Mrs. Tandy was trying to push her swollen feet back into her shoes.

Suddenly Sammy darted away from the others. He said, "I'm leaving NOW!

"Did you see their clubs?

"Did you see their tongues?

"Did you see their muscles?

"Did you hear their speeches?

"You couldn't understand them. For all we know, they could have been saying they plan to eat us at breakfast!

17

"I'm not going to have breakfast here. You'll find ME at the front door!"

And before they could stop him, he ran up the steps.

At the top of the steps he ran behind one of the big stone posts to hide.

It was pretty dark there.

He stepped down hard on something soft and bumpy.

Suddenly he felt his arms pinned against his body.

He was lifted off his feet, straight into the air.

He was frozen with fear.

He squeezed his eyes shut.

When he finally opened them, he found himself looking straight into a face with black paint on it.

He was the prisoner of a Maori warrior.

Chapter 3:
A Blood-Chilling Scream

In a few seconds, Sammy felt his feet back on the floor.

The warrior let go of his arms.

Then he patted Sammy on the back.

In a kind voice, he said, "Steady there, old chap. Are you quite all right?

"You landed on my bare toes when you came around that post.

"I may be limping about for a few days.

"I hope I didn't give you a scare, lifting you off my toes in the dark like that."

Sammy said, "You ... speak English!"

The Maori warrior said, "Oh, my, yes. New Zealand has been ruled by the English for nearly two hundred years.

"Our Maori language is only used at home, and for special friends. We mostly speak English, at school and at work."

Sammy said, "You work when you're not busy scaring people? What do you do?"

The Maori laughed. "I'm a panel beater. I fix dents in cars. You might call me an auto-body man in your country."

Sammy said, "Well, then, how come you're running around here looking like THAT?"

The man said, "We want to remember our old Maori customs. We want our children to know about our past."

Sammy said, "Then you don't have wars with those sticks anymore?"

The man smiled. "No, not for over a hundred years. Did we have you worried?"

Sammy said, "Well ... maybe a little. You don't ... kill your enemies?"

The man said, "No, although I must say I thought about it when you landed on my bare foot! You're a solid little chunk, my boy."

Sammy said, "And you don't ... you wouldn't ... EAT someone?"

The man laughed again and took hold

of Sammy's hand. He said, "What's your name?"

Sammy said, "Sammy."

The man said, "I'm Hohua." He said it like this: HOE-hoo-uh.

He said, "Let's have breakfast together. I promise not to take a bite out of you. But YOU must promise not to eat ME, either."

Hand in hand they walked to the tables at the other end of the museum.

The rest of the Woodlanders had come up the stairs.

When Sammy saw them he felt terrible.

He said, "Oh my gosh. I forgot to help Dave get up the stairs."

He ran over to them, dragging his new friend with him.

He said, "Sorry I ran out on you, Dave."

Then he pointed to the big man next to him. He said, "This is Hohua, my Maori friend.

"He won't hurt me, or you. And you guys better be nice to him because he's STRONG. He picked me up in the air."

Bill said, "STRONG! If you picked my brother up, you must be a forklift!"

They all sat down to breakfast together.

After breakfast they went to see the

Maori carvings with Hohua.

They saw big carved wooden heads with their eyes staring, and their tongues sticking straight out.

Hohua said, "When the tongue sticks straight out, it stands for hating an enemy. If it's bent to the side, it's a friendly tongue."

Right away Sammy stuck his tongue out at Bill. He said, "Now you can't get mad at me, Bill. My tongue is bent to the side."

There were giant carved wooden men in the show.

Hohua pointed at one and said, "How would you like to walk under that giant's legs! His legs used to be the doorway to a storehouse! He kept the things inside safe."

They saw some beautiful carved fish hooks.

Hohua said, "An old Maori story says that the North Island of New Zealand was pulled up from the sea on a magical fish hook. That's one reason fish hooks are so important to the Maori people."

They saw woven capes covered with

bright bird feathers.

Sammy ran up to a glass case full of clubs and sticks.

He said, "Look, Bill! Here's the best stuff! Here's what you can use if your enemy attacks!"

Sammy pointed to some short, flat clubs. Then he pretended to jab one right into Bill's belly. He hit Bill hard, with his fist!

Bill grabbed Sammy's hand. He said, "Hey! That museum guard is looking at you!"

But Sammy just giggled. He said, "Look at me, Hohua!"

He stuck his tongue out as far as he could. He made his eyes bulge like a Maori warrior's.

He bent his legs. He began to grunt and do a war dance, right near the display cases.

Hohua laughed, but the museum guard began walking toward them.

Bill grabbed Sammy's arm and steered him toward the door.

He said, "Bye, Hohua! Got to go! Come on, guys! It's time to head home and get some sleep!"

At 4:30 that afternoon, the Woodlanders were still asleep. But at 4:31 they were WIDE AWAKE!

They heard a blood-chilling scream.

It came from the garage.

It was Sammy.

Chapter 4:
The First Possum

Dave pulled himself out of his bed. He threw himself into his wheelchair.

Dave, Bill, Kathy, and Mrs. Tandy raced to the back door of the garage.

And there was Sammy.

He was standing on the hood of Dave's car.

He had a suitcase in each hand.

He shouted at them, "Watch out! Something's trying to kill me! It's hiding out on those shelves over there. Stay back!"

They heard a scratching noise.

Then they heard a hissing sound.

But they couldn't see anything.

Bill reached out and pressed the garage-door opener on the wall.

The big garage door went up.

Bill called to Sammy, "I'm heading over to you. When I'm near you, jump off the car, and we can run out that door together."

Dave said, "Don't worry, Bill. Sammy's OK. Come on, let's go look at that little fellow."

Sammy shouted, "Little fellow! Do you know what this thing is?"

Dave laughed. He said, "Sure! I've heard that hissing sound before. See, it's stopped. I bet it fainted. You're safe.

"Take a look at it. Is it a gray, furry little rat-nosed thing lying there, all curled up? With a bare, ratty tail?"

Sammy said, "Yes. How did you know? It sounded big. I thought it was going to get me.

"See, I decided to go to New Zealand with you guys after all. So I came out to get my suitcase. But then I thought I'd be dead before I could go. Eaten alive!"

Dave laughed. "You'd get into the *Guinness Book of Records* if that happened, Sammy. You'd be famous.

"Only person on record ever killed by a half-grown possum."

Kathy smiled. "Really, Sammy, he

won't hurt you unless you poke your finger in his face."

Sammy said, "Just the same, he sounded like he hated my guts."

They all went to look at the possum.

It was lying perfectly still on the shelf.

Its eyes were shut.

Its little tongue was hanging out a bit.

Kathy said, "That's a possum, all right. Did you know they have pouches, like kangaroos?"

Sammy said, "You're kidding! This thing doesn't look anything like a kangaroo."

Dave said, "No, but the mothers do have pouches. And they can have as many as twenty babies at one time.

"I saw in a book that the babies are so little, twenty would fit in a teaspoon. They're like little pink worms with front legs."

Sammy said, "Boy, speaking of worms, you're a worm, Dave. A bookworm. I bet you've read every book in the Bluff Lake Library."

Dave laughed. "Not quite, but here's another thing I found out. After they're born, those tiny things climb through their mother's fur.

"The ones that make it to her pouch stay there for ten weeks. Then they climb out and go for a ride on her back."

Sammy said, "No way! This is a trick to get me to like stinky old possums!"

Kathy said, "It's true, Sammy. And that's not all! The babies wrap their tails around the mother's tail, like little monkeys. That way they won't fall from her back when she goes for a walk."

Sammy said, "Even if all this is true, I don't care. I'm through with possums. I'm never going to let one near me again!

"They hiss, they have ratty faces, and ratty tails, and this one tried to kill me.

"Now let's go in. I'm going to start packing for New Zealand. After all, it's only a month away!"

Chapter 5: Another Possum

At last it was time to go to New Zealand.

The Woodlanders had just boarded a huge plane. The plane began to roll up the runway.

Sammy cried, "Hooray! Here we go!"

The rest of the museum group was seated near them. Next to Sammy sat a pointy-nosed woman in a fluffy gray coat. She said in a bossy voice, "There's no need to make such a fuss, young man.

"Just sit quietly. Children should be seen and not heard."

Sammy was so surprised, he didn't answer back for a change.

But Bill leaned across Sammy and said to her, "He's just excited about the trip. We all are."

A few minutes later the seat-belt sign went off. Bill decided to talk to the woman a little more. He said, "Didn't we meet you the day of the Maori breakfast party?"

She said, "I don't remember meeting you. If I had, I wouldn't BE here. I didn't know the museum was allowing CHILDREN on this trip!

"I must speak to the tour leader ... I think her name is Tina ... about keeping order here."

She got up from her seat at the end of the row. She walked toward the back of the plane.

Sammy felt bad. He followed her with

his eyes. He stuck his tongue out so far, it looked like a hot dog.

Mrs. Tandy, sitting next to Bill, smiled. She said, "You handled that very well, you two. She was so rude! She acts like she's the queen of the whole plane.

"I saw her name tag. It said Blossom Babberton!"

Sammy said, "Babber-ton? You mean Blabber-Tongue! Blossom Blabber-Tongue, that's her name!"

Bill said, "Blabber-Tongue? I love it." He started to giggle.

Then Sammy got the giggles.

Then Dave and Kathy broke out laughing.

And finally, so did Mrs. Tandy.

Mrs. Babberton came back.

She looked at Mrs. Tandy.

She said, "I can see why some children scream and scratch! They never have a chance to learn good manners from their mother!"

That was too much for Mrs. Tandy.

She said, "Excuse me, Mrs. Babberton. Before we start this two-week trip together, I have something to say to you.

"First of all, I'm Becky Tandy. And I'm not these kids' mother. I just wish I were.

"We all live together as a family. We call ourselves the Woodlanders.

"Now, I've known these kids for quite a while. From time to time they make a little noise ... so do I for that matter ... but I've NEVER seen them scream and scratch."

Then Mrs. Tandy said, "And now, if you'll excuse me, I have to get out to the restroom."

She stood up and made her way past Bill and Sammy.

Mrs. Babberton hissed as Mrs. Tandy squeezed past her.

Then she pulled her coat around her and curled against the seat. She closed her eyes and went to sleep so fast, it looked like she fainted.

Sammy said, "Wow! I've seen that before! Hissing, then fainting!"

"It looks like Blossom Blabber-Tongue is really POSSUM BLABBER-TONGUE!"

Bill laughed. "And I thought you said you were never going to let a possum get near you again!"

Just then a woman walked up. She stopped in an empty seat in front of them. She kneeled on it and faced them over the seat back.

Bill whispered, "Uh-oh! Here's Tina Chow, our trip leader. I bet Possum Blabber-Tongue warned her about us!"

But Tina Chow was smiling. She nod-

ded toward Mrs. Babberton.

She whispered, "Oh, I see she's gone to sleep. She told me you were up to no good ... that I'd have to keep an eye on you. But you look perfectly friendly to me!"

Bill said, "Thanks!"

Sammy said, "She's SO far off. We try

to help people. We solve mysteries, too!"

Tina Chow said, "Then I have a mystery to tell you about. There's an old Maori meeting house that was lost over a hundred years ago."

Kathy said, "Lost? How could anybody lose a house!"

Chapter 6: The Lost House

Sammy said, "Was this a really small house ... so small they lost it? Is it a DOLL house you're talking about?"

Tina Chow smiled and shook her

head. "The Maoris have built holy meeting houses for hundreds of years. Like the one at our museum.

"They built twelve of them at Tokomaru Bay at different times." She said it like this: TOKE-oh-mar-oo.

"The meeting house comes from there. There's only one left standing at Tokomaru Bay now. And it's only sixty years old."

Dave said, "Who builds them?"

Tina said, "The Maoris train their own carvers. The whole tribe, and friends of the tribe, all give money to build new meeting houses.

"To a Maori, a meeting house is like a person. Its face is at the top front, and the top board of the roof is its backbone. Each house even has its own name!"

Sammy said, "What were the names of

46

the ones at Tokomaru Bay?"

Tina laughed. She said, "Oh, Sammy, you'd never remember them all. But I'll write some of them down for you."

Sammy said, "Great! Write them into this notebook. My teacher said I have to get something into it every day of the trip."

Tina wrote these names:

Kiri kiri
Hiki hiki
Tu mo ka i
Ma u i
Re re ko hu

Sammy said, "Man! Those are real tongue-twisters!"

Dave said, "What about the mystery

house?"

Just then, Mrs. Tandy worked her way back to her seat. She said, "Hi, Tina! Mystery house? What am I missing here?"

Tina said, "Rerekohu is the house that ended up lost." She said the word like this: RAY-RAY-ko-hoo.

"It was built two hundred years ago. At that time another Maori tribe was at war with the tribe that owned it.

"The owners knew an attack was coming. They knew their enemies would chop up the carvings in the meeting house. That would be like killing the tribe's ancestors.

"So the tribe decided on a great plan.

"The next morning everyone set to work. They took the roof off of Rerekohu.

"They lifted its heavy carved posts out of the ground.

"They took the walls down, one board at a time.

"They took the whole house apart.

"They soaked all the pieces in whale oil until no water could ever hurt the wood.

"Then, in the middle of the night, they sneaked out of their camp.

"They took the pieces of the house to a river, not far away. They buried them in the wet riverbank."

Kathy cried out, "Buried them! In wet ground! Were the wood pieces still OK when they dug them out?"

Tina said, "That's just the trouble. The war went on for years. The river changed its course. Bushes and trees and small plants grew all over the old riverbed.

"Peace finally came. But by then, most of the people who had helped bury the house were dead. No one was sure where it was buried.

"They searched for many years. But they never found it."

Tina Chow stood up and said, "Well, I should get back to the others. See you later!"

Kathy said, "Thanks for telling us about Rerekohu."

Sammy said, "Uh-huh! Because now that we know about it, we are going to find it!"

Tina laughed. She said, "Maybe so, Sammy, but don't be too disappointed if you don't. The tribe gave up all hope of ever finding it long ago."

At last the plane landed in Auckland, on New Zealand's North Island.

The Woodlanders stood waiting for their bags. Suddenly a big black dog jumped onto the moving suitcase belt. He ran along sniffing every bag and box.

New Zealand

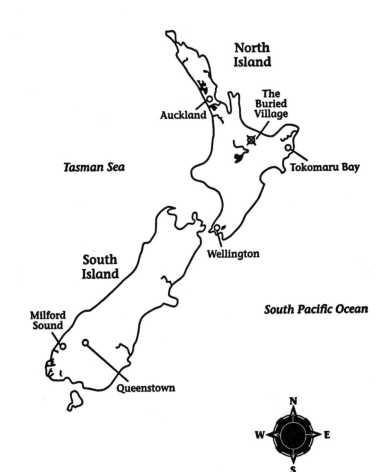

Sammy said, "Hey, someone catch that dog! He could get hurt up there!"

A police officer said, "He's all right, son. He's a police dog. He helps keep the airport safe. You know, sniffing for drugs and bombs."

In front of the airport, a woman was waiting for them.

She said, "Welcome to New Zealand. I'm Marina, your Maori guide."

Bill whispered, "Gosh, she's pretty!"

Sammy whispered, "Bill has a girlfriend ... Bill has a GIRLfriend."

The bus driver was standing next to Marina. He took a look at Mrs. Tandy. Then he walked up to her.

He said, "May I greet you with our Maori greeting, the HONGI?"

Mrs. Tandy nodded her head yes.

The driver leaned forward. He pressed his nose against hers, two times.

He said, "We share the breath of life in greeting. We do it once in memory of our ancestors. We do it again to honor each other."

Mrs. Tandy said, "I like that! The HONGI, you call it? I think I'll HONGI my way across New Zealand!"

The driver picked up her suitcase. He said, "May I help you aboard?" He held out his arm for her to lean on.

Now Sammy whispered, "Mrs. Tandy has a boyfriend ... Mrs. T. has a boyfriend."

Then Mrs. Babberton came up to Sammy and said, "No one is helping ME! I should be first! Here, you, boy, carry my bags on board."

And she put them down on either side of Sammy and got onto the bus.

Bill sang, "Sammy's got a girlfriend. Are you going to HONGI with her?"

Sammy turned as red as blood. He hooked his fingers into his mouth and pulled it wide. He made his killer-snake face at Bill, sticking his tongue in and out.

He whispered, "Old bossy Blabber-Tongue is NOT my girlfriend! She's not even a GIRL! Take that back, or I'll make you!"

He put up his fists.

Bill laughed. He said, "OK, OK, I take it back.

"Here, I'll help you put her bags on the bus. And then we can get Dave on. And our bags, too.

"But we better get going, if we are ever going to find the lost house!"

Chapter 7: This Is WAR!

Finally they were all on the bus.

They sank back against the soft sheep-skin seat covers.

Mrs. Babberton had taken the front

seat, near where Marina sat.

The bus started.

Blossom Babberton turned on a tape recorder.

Marina said, "First we will go to the hotel. You can get cleaned up and have breakfast there.

"Then we can explore by bus for about four hours.

"Our first stop will be the Buried Village!"

Kathy said, "Is that where Rerekohu is buried?"

Marina said, "Rerekohu! So you've been doing some homework! No, this is a whole town that got buried over a hundred years ago."

Sammy said, "If it's buried, how can we see it?"

Mrs. Babberton said, "Hush. I'm taping what our guide says."

Marina said, "Oh, no, Sammy, speak right up. That's a very good question. Much of the village IS still buried, but much has been dug out."

Bill asked, "What buried it in the first place?"

Mrs. Babberton said, "Oh, do be still."

Sammy moaned and whispered to Bill, "We have to be with Blabber-Tongue for this whole trip!"

Marina said, "I'm glad to answer all questions, Mrs. Babberton. That's what I'm here for.

"Here's the hotel now. But later on, Bill, I'll tell the whole story of the Buried Village."

Two hours later they were back on the bus.

They passed hundreds of hills.

Marina said, "These hills used to be volcanos that shot out lava."

They passed thousands of boats along the ocean coast.

They passed phone poles with metal wrapped around them.

Sammy said, "What's the metal stuff for?"

Marina said, "To keep possums from climbing to the top. They love to eat the covering on electric wires."

Sammy said, "POSSUMS! You have those mean old rat-tails here?"

Marina laughed. She said, "We have them, all right. I would hardly call them mean, but the electric company people would!

"And they aren't rat-tails. They're different from your possums. These have bushy tails and beautiful fur.

"And they're night animals. You almost never get to see them during the day."

Mrs. Tandy said, "Look at the sheep on those hills. They're as thick as ants at a picnic! How many ARE there in New Zealand, anyway?"

Marina said, "Seventy million sheep, but only three-and-a-half million people!

"If you think you're seeing a lot of sheep on North Island, wait till you see South Island! It's FULL of sheep. And mountains.

"Oh, look at that tree! It's called a cabbage tree, but it's really in the lily family."

Sammy said, "A tree? Like a lily? That's silly. Hey, I made a poem! I'll write it in my notebook. And I better write down what you tell us, too. And I'll keep a list of what I see. My teacher will love this."

He started writing.

cabbage trees... lily family
hills, all over
ocean, along a curvy shore
rivers
Kiwi fruit vines, like grape vines

farms
silver fern trees
sheep dogs, that don't bark
sheep, 35 kinds, Marina says
never scare sheep, they die of shock

Marina pointed to some giant trees. She said, "Those are called Kah-oor-ee trees. It's spelled K-A-U-R-I, Sammy.

"When those trees are hurt, they bleed a yellow sap. The sap runs into the soil.

"It turns hard, and people go around years later with steel rods, poking the soil to find chunks of it. It's called amber. It gets made into jewelry. It's very rare, and worth a lot of money."

Sammy said, "I want to find some amber! I'll poke all of New Zealand if I have to!"

Mrs. Babberton said, "You're a little fool. You'll spend so much time looking for tree sap, you'll miss everything else."

Mrs. Tandy saw Sammy's feelings were hurt.

She said, "Mrs. Babberton, it's not half as foolish as what YOU'RE doing. You'll spend your whole trip fooling with your tape recorder. You'll never see anything at all!"

The two women looked at each other, eyes shining with anger.

Sammy looked like a storm cloud. He whispered to Bill, "This is WAR!"

But just then Marina said, "Look!"

She pointed to a sign. It said BURIED VILLAGE. PARK HERE.

The bus stopped.

Mrs. Babberton jumped off. She hurried over to the tall wooden fence that hid the Buried Village.

She called back, "Hurry them up, Marina! I don't want to miss anything!"

But the park guard at the gate sent her back to the bus.

Sammy saw that and grinned.

He poked Bill in the ribs and said, "I'm keeping score. The Woodlanders against Possum Blabber-Tongue! And that's one point for our side!"

He opened to a page in his notebook. He drew a line down the middle.

At the top of one side he wrote WOODLANDERS.

At the top of the other side he wrote BLAB.

He put one mark on their side.

Then Marina called, "Everyone off the bus. Stay together, near me. It's time to hear the story of the Buried Village!"

Chapter 8:
The Buried Village

Inside the fence they saw more hills ...
more sheep ... and paths leading to huge
dug-out holes in the ground.

Dave said, "Wait a minute. The

ground is all grayish. It looks just like volcano ash. I saw a bottle of it in my earth-science class last year."

Marina said, "That's just what it is."

She pointed to a mountain. She said, "That volcano blew up one night. The ground we are standing on was a Maori town.

"No one knew the mountain was a volcano. When it blew, it covered the land with hot ashes ... two meters deep in some places. That's more than six feet deep!"

Sammy stamped his foot. He said,

"You mean there could be houses right under here?"

Marina said, "Yes. Houses, a church, a school, two hotels, animals, and people ... whole families, buried alive.

"It happened in the middle of the night. The earth was shaking. It woke people up. Along with the earthquake, the mountain exploded. Fire burst out of its top.

"Giant tongues of flame licked the sky. Lightning flashed again and again. Thunder boomed.

"Hot ashes fell like stinging rain. Balls of red-hot stone blew into the air and landed everyplace. Then something even worse happened."

Kathy said, "How could anything be worse than all that?"

Marina said, "A dark cloud of poison gas rolled slowly down the mountainside. By eleven in the morning most people were dead.

"One man wrote a letter while all this was happening. One line of it said, 'This is the most awesome moment of my life.'

"They found the letter next to his body, days later."

Bill said, "Wasn't there any warning before all this happened?"

Marina said, "Yes, but the English people said it was just silly Maori talk. The flax, our holy plant, had not bloomed the year before. Our leaders said there would be a dry summer and a huge earthquake.

"Then one day the lake water came up nearly a foot ... then went down quickly.

"Some English visitors were boating with some Maoris. They all saw a Maori war canoe coming out of the mist.

"It came so close the visitors could see the warriors, who were bowing their heads.

They wore white feathers in their hair.

"The visitors waved, but the war canoe disappeared into the mist.

"The Maoris rowing the visitors' boat began to shake and moan."

Dave asked, "Why? What was so bad about seeing that canoe?"

Marina said, "Because there WAS no war canoe. The Maoris knew there hadn't been one on the lake for years!"

Mrs. Tandy said, "My stars! Then you're talking about a ghost boat?"

Mrs. Babberton said, "Marina! Filling the heads of children with such silly stuff. Goodness knows these children are silly enough without it. No one with any brains believes in ghosts."

Marina said, "I don't believe in ghosts, either, Mrs. Babberton. But I do believe in telling the truth. I'm simply telling you the old Maori stories about the Buried Village."

Dave wheeled over to Mrs. Babberton. He said, "People believe in lots of things that you may not believe. But no matter what, you should be more polite to Marina."

Sammy said, "So, Dave, do YOU think they really saw a boat?"

Dave said, "I don't believe it, and I don't not believe it. I wasn't there. Things like that can't be proved. They aren't based on facts we can look at."

Mrs. Babberton was leaning back against a wire fence.

On the other side of the fence were several goats.

One of them, a big black male goat, was running back and forth, showing off for the female goats.

Mrs. Babberton said, "Young man, I don't believe in ghosts any more than I believe I can FLY."

As she said those words, the big goat saw her leaning against the fence.

He raced up and butted her ... HARD.

And Blossom Babberton FLEW!

She flew through the air toward Bill. He caught her and held her steady as she landed.

Sammy whispered, "That's another point for the Woodlanders.

"I guess I don't really believe in ghosts.

"Mrs. Babberton doesn't believe in ghosts.

"But, boy, after today I bet she believes in GOATS!"

Chapter 9:
Sammy's Ten-Day Diary

Tina Chow spoke to the museum group at dinner that night. "In ten days we will meet again with the Maoris who came to the museum for our party. At that time we will go to Tokomaru Bay."

Sammy said, "Why ten days? I can't wait to see my friend Hohua! And start looking for the buried meeting house. Can't we go right away?"

Tina said, "Here's the plan. First we learn everything we can about New Zealand, and about Maori life."

Sammy said, "What is this, school or something?"

Tina said, "No, Sammy. We want the Maoris to know how much we respect them. Then they might be more likely to help us."

Kathy said, "Help us? Help us do what?"

Tina said, "The Maori meeting house in the museum is falling apart. We need the Maoris' help to re-build it. Perhaps if we learn their ways, they will trust us. And help us."

That was the start of a stuffed-full ten days.

Sammy wrote every night in his notebook.

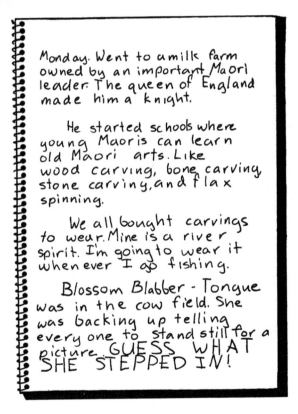

Monday. Went to a milk farm owned by an important Maori leader. The queen of England made him a knight.

He started schools where young Maoris can learn old Maori arts. Like wood carving, bone carving, stone carving, and flax spinning.

We all bought carvings to wear. Mine is a river spirit. I'm going to wear it whenever I go fishing.

Blossom Blabber - Tongue was in the cow field. She was backing up telling every one to stand still for a picture GUESS WHAT SHE STEPPED IN!

Tuesday. We visited three
different Maori tribes.
Every tribe danced and
made speeches and food.
I'm stuffed!

Wednesday. A Maori tribe invited us to spend the night in their meeting house. Young women did dances. And they twirled small white balls on strings. We all sang.

Then they brought out piles of clean sheets and mattresses. About fifty of us slept in the meeting house. We talked all night. It was the biggest pajama party ever.

The next day Blabber-Tongue bragged that she had sneaked her tape recorder in. But when she played it, there were just scratching noises. Hah!

Thursday. We went swimming in warm springs owned by a Maori tribe. Then they showed us how to weave. We made balls and fish shapes out of palm leaves. I'll show the class how, with cattail leaves back home.

Friday. We flew in a small plane to Wellington, the capital city! I got to sit right behind the pilot. Bill sat behind the co-pilot. We watched everything they did.

Then we took a huge ferryboat across to the South Island. We watched a woman spinning yarn. Mrs. Tandy got really interested. She ordered a spinning wheel shipped home to Bluff Lake.

The Maoris landed here at least 700 years ago. The English came hundreds of years later.

But the woman in the spinning shop said that Maori children used to be whipped. Why? For speaking Maori instead of English in school.

Saturday. We took another small plane to Queenstown. I told the pilots I'd help them if they needed me. They said they didn't think they would. I sat right behind them just in case.

Marina was right. South Island is all MOUNTAINS! We went to a sheep ranch and saw them give a sheep a haircut. They call it shearing. All the hairs come off stuck together, in one piece. It's called fleece.

If the fleece covers the sheep's eyes, the sheep won't move. It stops thinking. That's why people say, "He pulled the wool over my eyes."

Sunday. Today we went fishing and a

storm came up. We could hardly get back to shore. But today something even more exciting happened! I discovered SAUSAGE ROLLS. Little sausages baked in pie crust!

Now I am a sausage roll vampire!

Give me sausage rolls!

Monday. We spent the morning riding down a scary mountain road to Milford Sound. Boy, there's no use trying to tell you how skinny that road was. Or how twisty. Or how slippery. Or how steep the drop-offs were.

On the mountainsides were shiny

strips. I thought they were silver. But then I saw they were waterfalls, hundreds of feet long.

We got to Milford Sound in the rain. Mrs. Blabber-Tongue said she had paid for a boat ride, and was going to take it.

The rest of us stayed and played checkers. She came back looking like a wet rat. Or possum.

Tuesday. We went to a carving school. I think I've seen ten thousand Maori wooden carvings by now. I'm going to try to make one when I go home, out of balsa wood. Bill said he'd help me.

We ate mutton birds at a restaurant. Only Maoris are allowed to catch the little things. They eat them roasted.

Ours had been soaked in salt and oil. I pretended to like them, because I didn't want to look stupid. But here's how they tasted. YUCK!

Wednesday. A huge Maori breakfast, lunch, and tea. No one could eat dinner. Except me. We are stuffed full of Maori food and Maori ideas.

I won't be writing tomorrow. BECAUSE TOMORROW, AT LAST, WE GO TO TOKOMARU BAY!

Chapter 10:
The Underground Cook-out

It was early Thursday morning, at last!
At 5:00 A.M. the Woodlanders boarded a
plane.

They took two more short hops, on

tiny planes. Then they boarded a bus ... to Tokomaru Bay!

Finally, at 2:00 that afternoon, they stood in front of the meeting house at Tokomaru Bay. They sagged down onto benches set out for them.

Mrs. Tandy said, "My, I feel like we've been riding for a week!"

Sammy said, "More like a year!"

They were tired ... and hungry.

But Hohua and the other Maori men were lined up to greet them.

They were dressed as warriors.

Sammy groaned, "Oh, no! Not again!" as the warriors began to dance.

Then the Maoris made speeches.

And they sang a song after each speech.

And then the museum people made speeches.

Toward the end, Sammy was asleep,

sitting up, and snoring out loud.

Marina shook him gently and announced, "It will be three hours until the dinner feast. Maybe you'd like to go for a walk to a place I know about."

THAT WOKE SAMMY UP!

He jumped to his feet. He said, "Three hours! I'll be dead by then, Marina! I'm starving NOW!"

Bill said, "Come on, Sammy. You'll make it. Here, I've got pretzels from lunch."

Sammy said, "Pretzels! You rotten little piggy! How come you have pretzels and I don't?"

Bill said, "Because you ate your pretzels, and I saved mine. So YOU'RE the rotten little piggy."

Marina laughed.

Sammy filled both hands with pretzels and stuffed them into his mouth.

Bill said, "Let's find out what those men are doing over there."

Bill, Sammy, and Marina walked over to a huge hole dug into the ground.

It was about as big around as a car, but not as deep.

It was filled with glowing hot coals and stones. Metal racks lay on the stones.

The Maoris were covering the racks with bundles wrapped in leaves.

Dave, Kathy, and Mrs. Tandy came over to look.

Kathy said, "What is all this? Are they burning garbage?"

Marina smiled. "Oh, no! These Maoris are making a big HANGI for us."

Mrs. Tandy said, "A HANGI? I thought that was touching noses!"

Marina said, "That's the HONGI! This is the HANGI!"

The Maoris pulled pieces of rough brown cloth out of buckets of water. They lay the cloth on top of the leaf bundles in the pit.

Sammy said, "Ugh. Those look like old wet potato sacks."

Dave said, "That's what they are. Burlap sacks."

Bill said, "What exactly is a HANGI?"

Marina said, "It's a dinner, with everything cooked underground."

Sammy yelled, "A dinner! You're kidding! You can't get dinner out of a hole in the ground!"

Marina said, "Yes you can, and it will be wonderful! The food is inside those leaf bundles. Wait till you taste it!"

Then the cooks poured more water onto the burlap sacks.

The water sizzled and steam began to rise.

Other Maoris rushed to cover the wet sacks with big cloth tarps.

Now some men began throwing big shovels full of mud onto the tarps.

Thump ... thump.

Sammy said, "This makes me sick.

"We are supposed to eat food wrapped in leaves ... and hidden under old bags ... and sloshed with water ... and filled with smoke ... and covered with tarps ... and buried under mud?

"Forget it. Give me the rest of the pretzels, Bill. You can eat the food at the HANGI. Not me."

Bill said, "If I know you, you'll eat it. But it won't be ready for about three hours. So let's go for that walk!"

Marina said, "Oh, I never got to tell you about where I'm sending you. It's a place of mystery ... about two blocks away from here.

"You walk down that road, past those old houses, past that block of old wooden buildings with stores in them.

"You'll come to a dried-out riverbed, some really bumpy land that drops down from the side of the bridge.

"It's filled with wild growth ... tall grasses and weeds and bushes and trees.

"They say that an old meeting house is buried there ... the one Kathy was asking about on the bus."

Sammy shouted, "Rerekohu! We heard about it two weeks ago, from Tina. We

92

were going to look for it. You mean you even know where we should start? WHAT ARE WE WAITING FOR?"

The rest of them grabbed shovels from a pile. With Bill pushing Dave, they raced down the road toward the old riverbed.

Sammy grabbed a shovel and raced after them yelling, "Wait for me! I'm your leader!"

Chapter 11:
The Horse Rescue

They raced along for two blocks.

Sammy caught up with Bill and Dave. He helped push the wheel chair up and down the curbs.

They passed the houses and stores. Finally they got to the bridge. They saw the wild, scrubby land.

Sammy waved a shovel in the air and called out, "Rerekohu! I'm coming!"

Mrs. Tandy said, "Let's go!"

And then they saw the horse.

A bony old horse was pulling against a rope tied to her neck. She was standing in grass up to her belly.

The rope was long.

But she was tied to a phone pole, and the pole had two wires running to the ground on each side. The horse had caught her rope in the wires!

Her hind leg was caught in loops of rope.

She looked scared.

She had a wild look in her eyes.

She jumped.

She tripped.

She snorted.

She tried to throw her head up into the air.

She danced sideways a little.

Dave said, "She's going to break a leg if we don't do something."

Kathy was already inching toward the animal. She was talking to the horse softly, and holding out a big bunch of grass for her to eat.

The horse backed away, but she kept looking at Kathy and the grass.

Kathy moved a step closer.

The horse began to kick.

Then she rose up on her hind legs. She waved her front legs in the air. Then she stood still for a moment.

Kathy began talking to her again.

Dave told Bill, Sammy, and Mrs. Tandy to talk softly and inch toward the horse, too.

He said, "She might get used to you after a while, if you don't make any sudden moves. Then one of you will be able to catch her rope near her head.

"When that happens, be sure the others all grab hold, too, in case she tries to buck up again."

Mrs. Tandy said softly, "Whatever you do, don't walk behind her. Remember, cows kick forward, horses kick backward."

The horse kept looking from one of them to the other.

Every few minutes one of them got a little closer before the horse backed away.

This went on for over an hour!

Finally the horse moved toward the grass that Kathy held out to her.

Kathy took hold of the rope. At that moment, three other pairs of hands took hold, too.

Dave had worked his way down the slope, close enough to feed the horse from a pile of grass on his lap. The others worked to free the animal.

The only tool they had was Sammy's little fishing knife.

They sawed away at the thick rope while the blue sky turned gray-blue.

They sawed away at the rope through the silver-pink clouds of sunset.

It was almost dark before they sawed

through the last bit of rope.

Sammy put his knife away. He looked all around and saw how dark the sky was. He said, "Well, this sure killed our chances of finding the buried house.

"But saving a horse is pretty important, too."

Dave said, "It's lucky we came down here when we did. I wonder who tied her there."

They all took turns leading the horse back to the meeting house. She followed them easily.

Mrs. Tandy said, "I bet she's happy to be free. I think she likes us."

Marina saw them walk up with the horse.

She laughed and said, "I thought you were looking for a HOUSE, not a HORSE. Where did you find it?"

Mrs. Babberton was standing near them. She said, "I knew those children would get into trouble. Just imagine! Stealing someone's horse."

Just then a Maori man ran up. He said, "Why do you have my animal?"

Mrs. Babberton said, "Now you're in for it."

Dave said, "She was all caught up in some wire and bushes. She could have hurt herself. We got her quiet, and then cut her free."

The man said, "Thank you. That was very kind of you. And brave. Let me take her and tie her up in a safer place. The HANGI is ready now."

The food was laid out on tables.

A wonderful smell filled the air. Sammy began sniffing around like the police dog at the airport. He went from one pile of leaves to another, sniffing.

At last he said, "I take back what I said. This stuff smells great! Count me in!"

Bill said, "I TOLD you you'd eat it."

Sammy just stuck out his tongue. Sideways.

They ate lamb and chicken. They ate vegetables, fruit, and home-made bread.

Then Mrs. Tandy saw a dish full of yellow slippery things, shaped like tiny tongues. She saw a Maori woman put one onto a piece of bread, and swallow it. So she did, too, and so did all the Woodlanders.

It was the insides of sea urchins, and Sammy HATED it!

He made a face and said, "Ugh! This tastes like medicine! Everything else was great, though. I'm going to dig a cooking hole in our yard in Bluff Lake, and make my own HANGI."

Now the time had come for Tina Chow to ask the Maoris for help in rebuilding the museum's meeting house.

Sammy whispered to Bill, "Boy, I wish we'd been able to find Rerekohu for them. I bet they would have helped us then!"

They all took off their shoes and slowly headed into the meeting house.

Chapter 12:
One Last Try

The visitors and the Maoris all sat on mattresses.

The first Maori stood and spoke.

He said, "I say we should not help the Americans re-build the other house.

"That house is too far away.

"It might not be given respect."

Another Maori rose. "That house should be brought back here or left alone.

"I know for a FACT, people from the museum DON'T know how to respect holy houses.

"Even tonight one of them brought shame to herself in this meeting house. Against our rules she was hiding a tape recorder. I had to stop her."

He looked right at Blossom Babberton. She curled up on her mattress. In one second she seemed to be asleep.

Dave looked over at Tina Chow. Arms and legs crossed, she was sitting as still as a statue, listening to every word.

She was trying to keep her face calm, but Dave could tell she was disappointed.

Then the horse's owner got up. He

said, "I have something to say."

He pointed to the Woodlanders. "That group of young people, and that woman with them, showed me that we CAN trust these museum people."

Everyone turned to look at them.

Kathy's face turned as red as an apple.

The man went on. "This afternoon my horse got mixed up in her rope.

"Marina tells me that these people had planned a fine adventure. But instead, they spent their hours saving my poor old horse.

"They proved to me they are loving and kind people.

"I believe they and most of their friends would also be kind to the spirits of the meeting house.

"I say we should help them re-build it."

And by the end of the meeting, that is what the Maoris decided.

After the meeting, the Maoris talked about the rescue of the horse.

One woman said she thought the Woodlanders had been very brave.

One man said he would find it hard to go near such a big animal when it was frightened.

They all laughed when they heard that the Woodlanders had planned to look for Rerekohu.

One man said, "Remember this, my children and my dear lady ... our ancestors searched long and hard for Rerekohu. Don't feel like you've failed in not finding it."

A woman said, "If this meeting is over, it's time for Becky Tandy and the others to help make a special dessert.

"Sammy bragged about how good their

oatmeal cookies are at home. So I made them promise to show me how to make them!"

Everyone filed out of the meeting house and put on their shoes.

The Woodlanders spent an hour in the kitchen. Then they brought out the oatmeal cookies.

Problems solved, stomachs full, everyone finally went back into the meeting house to sleep.

Early the next morning, Bill woke up.

A terrible taste filled his mouth.

Something awful had dropped onto his tongue.

He sat straight up.

He spit it out into his hand.

Then he saw Sammy's grinning face.

Bill looked down into his hand. There was a pile of the medicine-tasting sea urchin stuff!

Bill whispered, "Sammy, I should mash you into a pancake!"

Sammy whispered back, "Shh ... I was just trying to wake you up without waking anyone else up.

"Anyway, I was thinking, we don't have to leave until after breakfast. I was thinking we could make one last try, to find Rerekohu."

Bill said, "And the only way you could think of to wake me up was with THIS?"

He jumped out of bed ... and wiped the spit-out sea urchin juice onto Sammy's jeans.

The other Woodlanders were awake by now.

They all got dressed.

In the near-dark morning they sneaked out of the meeting house and put on their shoes.

They headed down to the old riverbed with some shovels.

The sun was just coming up.

The air was cool.

Bill said, "This air is nippy."

Sammy said, "And you are drippy."

Then Bill said, "You're pretty lippy."

Kathy said, "This road is dippy."

Dave threw in, "And my chair is tippy!"

And Mrs. Tandy said, "And having to think of the last rhyme isn't fair!"

Bill smiled and said, "We did use up most of the good rhymes."

At the dried-up riverbed, Dave said,

"Look, guys, I'm not going down to hunt with you. The ground is so bumpy, I'd only slow you down.

"Yesterday my chair almost tipped a couple of times when I tried to help with the horse.

"I'll stay up on the edge while you hunt."

Kathy said, "Then why don't you tell us where to hunt? You can see where we are from up here. Keep us from going over the same ground twice."

Dave said, "OK. How about starting right under the bridge?"

They walked down to where he pointed, in among the wild bushes.

He called, "Just dig where you're standing, and then work your way to my right."

But just then Sammy yelled out, "HEY! LOOK OVER THERE! WHAT IS IT?"

Chapter 13:
The Final Possum

Sammy started running.

He darted through the bushes of the old riverbed.

He waved his shovel and yelled, "I see

one! I see one! It's a New Zealand possum! I'm going to follow it! Come on, guys!"

He forgot all about Rerekohu.

He raced through the thorny weeds.

He tripped over tree roots.

Finally he fell.

When he picked himself up, the possum was gone.

But he kept pushing through the bushes.

He thought he knew which way the possum had run.

Bill yelled to the others, "Sammy could get hurt! There are thorns and holes all over the place! He could even get lost!"

They began to race after Sammy.

Finally Sammy was across from Dave, about a football field away.

Suddenly he realized he couldn't hear the others. He stopped.

He felt scared.

From above Dave had seen everything.

He began to wave wildly. He shouted, "SAMMY! STAY WHERE YOU ARE! KEEP MAKING NOISE AND THE OTHERS WILL FIND YOU!"

Sammy heard Dave and felt better. He waved back and grinned.

He sat down near two tall trees.

He said loudly, "Make noise, huh? I'm good at that!

"Oops. I wonder if there are any snakes here." He began to feel crawly. "Oh. Right. No snakes in New Zealand."

He started singing, "The ants go marching one-by-one ... " but that made him feel crawly again.

So he started poking the ground with a stick to see if he could find any amber.

He sang, "I've been working on the

railroad ... " He turned up something interesting with his stick.

It was a flat piece of shell. It was about as big as a person's ear, and leaf-shaped.

It had a small hole in the middle of it.

Sammy shouted, "Hey! This is great! It will remind me of the day I saw a New Zealand possum ... and ran faster than Bill!"

Just then Mrs. Tandy, Kathy, and Bill

broke through the bushes. There was so much hugging, Sammy was afraid he'd lose his shell. He stuck it into his pocket to protect it.

Dave shouted down, "Good work, guys! Do you want to keep looking for the house?"

They all shouted yes.

Dave said, "OK! Well, you can't search the whole riverbed, it's so big. You might as well start working where you are now.

"Why don't you walk toward me? Stop and dig about every twenty feet."

By the time they reached Dave, it was time for breakfast.

Then Sammy remembered his shell. He pulled it out to show them.

He said, "Look. I found this old piece of shell! But I sure wish we had found the old meeting house instead."

Mrs. Tandy said, "Well, we gave it our best shot. The old house was just too smart for us."

But Dave said, "My gosh, Sammy! Where did you find this!"

Sammy said, "Right by where I was sitting, waiting for these slowpokes. It was in the ground. Near those big trees." He pointed. "Let's see, were those the ones?"

Dave's face broke out in a big grin. He said, "Those ARE the ones, Sammy! And we have to get markers on them. Now!"

He quickly took off his shirt. He said, "Bill, I need your shirt, too."

Bill said, "Sure, but what's going on?"

Dave said, "Look at this shell thing. It didn't just grow this way.

"Someone cut it to make this shape.

"And someone drilled this hole in it.

"And look how dirty it is. It was buried under the ground. Somehow, through the years, it worked up to the top.

"You know what it is? I'd bet my life this is one of those eyes made of shell! An eye from a meeting house!

"Sammy, I think you've found a buried eye ... from Rerekohu!"

Sammy started dancing, knees bent, chest out, Maori-style.

Bill started hitting him on the back and dancing with him.

Mrs. Tandy said, "Well, someone has to put up these markers!" So she and Kathy went back down to the riverbed.

They hung a shirt on a branch of each tree.

Then they all raced back to the Maoris and the meeting house.

Sammy held up the shell eye.

The Maoris crowded around to see it.

Sammy said, "I was going to keep this, but I think it's yours."

They knew what it was right away.

People cried, "Rerekohu! You found it! I can't believe it!" Everyone wanted to run right down to the riverbed.

But Hohua and an older Maori leader had other ideas. Hohua said, "We need to feed our guests before their bus comes. They have a long trip home ahead of them!"

The other man said, "Marina, please call the Auckland museum for us. We will need help digging. We don't want to hurt what is buried here.

"Then we will mark this day with a special feast ... to honor Rerekohu, our ancestors, and our visitors. Let's eat breakfast near the riverbed.

"When the time comes we can flag down the bus there.

"Now, everybody, pick up suitcases, and dishes, and bowls of food."

He picked up his carved cane. "And follow me!"

One by one, in a long parade, they walked toward the bridge.

Hohua cried, "It's the Rerekohu Finding Day March!"

They spread tablecloths on the grass above the riverbed.

After breakfast, the old leader walked up to Dave.

He said, "The members of our group have a gift for the Woodlanders. We will remember what you have done. We will always welcome you and your friends.

"Because you live half the world away, we want you to keep this. It is to remind you that you're in our hearts for ever."

He handed his carved cane to Dave.

Mrs. Babberton was sitting on the other side of the table cloth.

She called out, "Sir, you'll just have to say that all over again. My tape recorder was too far away to pick it all up."

She stood up and ran toward him.

But her foot came down in a bowl of sugar.

And her other foot slid into a plate of butter.

And both her legs flew out from under her.

She landed bottom first on the big plate of sea urchin insides.

She wasn't hurt, but WAS SHE MAD!

AND DID SHE SMELL!

Everyone felt like laughing, but they were all too polite.

A few people helped her up.

Steaming mad, she picked up one of her suitcases. She stomped into the bushes to change her clothes.

Sammy took out his notebook.

He wrote this:

Possum Blabber-Tongue scored this time. She found a perfect use for the sea urchin stuff. That's one point I'm glad to give her side.

Then one of the women held up a huge plastic bag. In it were oatmeal cookies left over from the night before.

So the Woodlanders and their friends talked and laughed and ate cookies in the bright New Zealand sun.